I don't know what this says, but it looks VERY boring!!!!

Scholastic Children's Books
An imprint of Scholastic Ltd
Euston House, 24 Eversholt Street
London, NW1 1DB, UK
Registered office: Westfield Road, Southam, Warwickshire, CV47 0RA
SCHOLASTIC and associated logos are trademarks and or registered trademarks of Scholastic Inc.

First published in the UK by Scholastic Ltd, 2016

ISBN 978 1407 1 5527 2

A CIP catalogue record for this book
is available from the British Library.

Printed and bound by CPI Group (UK) Ltd, Croydon, CR0 4YY

1 3 5 7 9 10 8 6 4 2

www.scholastic.co.uk

Me I is Pig. I has totally lost count of
how old I is. I thinks I is the biggest I can
be, so that must make
me oldish, but I still has
some very silly thoughts,
so I thinks
that I must
also be quite
young.

   I lives on **Mr and Mrs Sandal's farm**
with my best friend **Duck**, my most lovely
friend **COW** and all the **Sheeps**. I has always
lived here – well, nearly. I made a bit
of a mistake not so long ago and we all
ended up living at an **Old Farmers'**
Home. The **Old Farmers** was very

nice, but it wasn't the same as living here. I asked for someone to tell **Mr and Mrs Sandal** where we was so they could rescue us, and they did! Amazing. I is wishing I is knowing who told them so I could be thanking them.

Anyways, we is back and we is all VERY happy. I never wants to leave the **Farm** or the **Sandals** again!

Mr and Mrs Sandal is so great – I loves them very much. They is Vegytarian. This is meaning that they is not wanting to eat me, which is a very good thing. I bets no one would be wanting to live with someone what is wanting to gobble them up. My last owner, **Farmer**, wanted to eat me, and this made me feel very sad and quite angry.

I is not sure what I loves about them the most. There is so many things. **Mrs Sandal** gives me the best back scratches. **Mr Sandal** sings funny songs to me. And they both feeds me the best-tasting slops ever. OK, that is a little bit of a lie – clearly I is loving slops the best, but I thinks if I says this it will make me look like a greedy Pig. So I is going to pretend that the other things is just as important.

Now we is back on the **Farm**, I lives in Pig House again. My house is

great; it's full of straw. Every night I
makes myself a special Piggy nest to sleep
in. The only thing what would make it
more perfect would be a pillow. I rests my
head on my trotters and sometimes when
I wakes up they feels all tingly. My head is
very heavy, you see.

My house is just across from my best
friend **Duck's**. I loves **Duck** very much, but
I doesn't want him to think I is a softie

Pig, so I has never told him. Duck lives in
a small house in the middle of **Duck Pond**.
I can't tell you what it is like inside 'cos
firstly I is not being able to swim, so I can't
get to it, and secondly I is much too big to
fit through his front door. BOO!

My friend **COW** lives across from me
in **cow shed**. Behind **cow shed** is the
veggie patch. I was a naughty Pig once and
got into it and, by mistake, ate all the

veggies. This made **Mr and Mrs Sandal** very cross and sad. I is never going to upset them ever, ever again.

Duck says the **Sandals** now grows a special kind of veggie what is called organik. He says this means they is super expensive so the **Sandals** gets lots more money when they sells them. Why would anyone wants

money more than they wants veggies?
Money doesn't taste anywhere near as nice
as veggies.

Apart from loving slops, my friends and
the Sandals, I also loves writing diaries. My
friend **COW** gave me this one.

COW is loving to play hide-and-seek. We
only found out about this recently, but
now we knows, she wants us to play it with
her **ALL** the time.

One day **COW** was trying to hide herself
down the back of the old armchair what Mr
Sandal keeps by the veggie patch. He sits on
it and sings to his veggies. I wonders if this
is what makes them organik? **Duck** says he
sings songs to them about growing big and

plump. The songs must work 'cos when **Mr Sandal** pulls up the veggies they looks VERY big and VERY plump. Ha! Ha!

Anyways, **COW** was busy squeezing herself down the back of the armchair when she found this little book. She is knowing that I loves my diaries so she gave it to me. **COW** is super nice like that.

So here it is, my number three diary. My other two diaries was quite bonkers. I is really not sure it is possible for this one to be bonkers as well 'cos all I has to write about is just me, **Duck** and **cow** playing on the **Farm**. So, I has decided to call it . . .

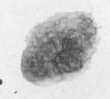

The Seriously Ordinary diary of Pig

Playday

Hello.

I is super happy to tell you that today was a good day.

It started with **Mrs Sandal** bringing me an enormous bowl of slops. This was sooooooo tasty that my tongue felt like doing happy somersaults in my mouth.

After breakfast I went over to see **Duck**. **Duck** is my best friend in the whole wide world. When bad things happens to me, **Duck** helps me out. And I knows I would do anything to help him – that's what being best friends is all about.

Duck is good at speaking other languages,

unlike me, and he is also really good at
making up games. Today we invented a
game called "Name That Fart". Basically,
I does a fart and **Duck** has to guess
what animal it sounds like. For starters I
squeezes my bottom cheeks together and
does this little squeaky one what kind of
goes "eeeek-eeeeeeek". **Duck** guesses straight
away: mouse. My bottom is very clever and
so is **Duck**.

I has just done my best ever fart impression of a donkey when **COW** comes over. **COW** is very funny, though I is not sure she is knowing it. **COW** doesn't know many words in Pig, and the ones what she does know, she sometimes gets a bit mixed up.

"**where's woc?**" she says.

"**WOC**" is "**COW**" said backwards, and "**where's woc?**" is her name for hide-and-seek. She calls it this because she only likes doing the hiding bit. She's getting really good at it. I has no idea how she manages to climb so high

or squeeze herself into such tiny spaces. She is amazing.

"OK," I says. I is actually quite happy to change games; I has almost run out of farty animal noises.

Me and **Duck** has to cover our eyes and count to one hundred. Then we shouts, "Coming, ready or not!!!"

(OK, I will tell you a secret here. I is not great at counting over ten, so I just makes noises what sound like the number **Duck** is saying. I fools him every time.)

Today **COW** is doing her best hiding yet. We searches for her for ages. We looks inside the bag what is on the back of the lawnmower, up the tree behind my house

and on top of the straw bales in the New
Barn. We is about to give up when I hears
"snore, snore, snore" coming from
the **Sandals'** wheelbarrow. Wheelbarrows is
not usually snoring. It must be **COW**! We
turns it over and there she is! We has
found her! Ha! Ha! She's all
tucked up in a very
uncomfortable-
looking ball, fast
asleep.

SNORE!
SNORE!

"Wake up, **COW**. We've found you!" I
shouts in her hairy **COW** ear. **COW'S** big

eyes opens and she looks a bit confused. I thinks she must have been in the middle of a big dream – probably about playing more **where's woc?** When she tries to stand up, her legs is not working properly 'cos they has been squashed underneath her. This makes her walk very funny.

Wibble-wobble-wibble-wobble goes **COW** as she walks back across the yard to her shed.

We all laughs so much, big tears runs down our faces. **COW'S** tears is HUGE!

Hummyday

Hello.

Today my brain is having a very good idea.

This morning there is a whole carrot in my bowl of slops. This is not usual; normally they is all mashed up. My tummy says, "Eat it! Eat it!" but then I has an amazing idea! I will sing to it and see if I can make it even bigger, just like **Mr Sandal** does!

So, I takes the carrot to the back of my

house, digs a little hole and
stuffs it into the soil.

I clears my throat and
I sings it a little song using my very best
singing voice. I sings quietly 'cos I doesn't
want **Duck** hearing. **Duck** is not saying nice
things about my singing voice. He is so rude
sometimes. He is also not a veggie genius
like I is — a Vegenius. Ha! Ha! Ha!

My Vegenius song goes:

I'd be a happy Pig, a happy Pig, a
happy Pig,
    If you, lovely Carrot, would grow
twice and big, twice as big.

I finishes and looks at the carrot. I is sure the stalk has grown a teensy bit taller already. If I could be patting myself on the back for being super clever I would, but my trotters isn't bending around that far.

I goes over and sits with **Duck**. 'Cos I is singing to my breakfast rather than eating it, I is not windy enough to play any farty games, so instead we watches **Mr and Mrs Sandal** working in their veggie patch. They is very good at growing veggies, so good that they grows more than they can eat. Every day they packs up the extra ones into big boxes and sends them to other **Farmers**. These boxes must be super strong 'cos veggies is weighing a lot. I knows this because when I eats lots I feels VERY HEAVY.

Each box has some **Farmer** words on it and a picture of **Mr and Mrs Sandal** smiling and holding some turnips. I is not surprised they is smiling. Turnips is the best-tasting veggie ever, followed by cabbyages and then potatoes. **Mr and Mrs Sandal** writes on each box, so the lorry knows where to take them.

At the end of every day a big lorry comes and collects them. **Duck** says the lorries delivers the veggie boxes all over the world. I is not really sure how big the world is, but when **Duck** says the word "**world**" he spreads his wings really wide, so I is guessing it must be pretty big.

I is so jealous of all the **Farmers** what gets to eat the **Sandal's** organik veggies. My tummy starts to rumble, so I goes back to my shed and sings to my carrot again. I shall grow an ENORMOUS super-tasty organik carrot, all for me.

Tragiday

Hello.

Today has not been a good day. In fact today has been a terrible day.

It didn't start being a terrible day. It started being a good day. It began with a very good veggie sing-song. This morning I added some really nice new words to make the carrot feel extra-extra special, and make it grow extra-extra big.

Oh, Carrot, you is so beautiful, orange and yummy!

Please get bigger, fatter and even more scrummy!

I so wants to dig it back up and see if it
has got any bigger. But I knows I is going
to have to be patient — which is very hard
when you loves veggies as much as I do.

Instead I goes over to **Duck Pond**.
COW is there already. "**WOC
has big parsnip**," she says.

I check, but **COW** is not
carrying a parsnip, which
is a shame. I thinks she
must mean she has a good
idea. In Pig, a big parsnip
is always a good idea — 'cos
parsnips is YUMMY. And I bets I know what
her good idea is: **where's woc?**

I is right. **COW** is VERY excited about

13

today's game. I knows when **COW** is excited
'cos she wiggles her bottom from side to
side. This morning her bottom is going
bonkers! When **COW** gets this excited it
means she has thought of a really great
place to hide.

I has to say, **COW'S** wiggly bottom is
looking very muscly today. In fact **COW** is
looking pretty muscly all over. It must be all
the climbing, bending and walking she's doing
playing **where's woc?** all the time.

I does my special sneaky counting thing
and we sets off to find her. We looks
everywhere we can think. **COW** was right
to be excited; she really has found a
difficult hiding place.

Just as we is rechecking under the big flowerpot in the **Sandals'** garden, I hears a low, sad **COW**-sound coming from above us.

I looks up. There on the roof of the **Sandals'** house, holding on to the chimney, is **COW**. I wonders how she got all the way up there.

"**hoooooooolp!**" she whimpers.

"Don't be worrying, **COW**," I shouts up.
"We'll rescue you!"

I has no idea how we is going to do this; I
just says it to stop her feeling scared. **Duck**
could fly up, but I doesn't have wings – and
Duck is not strong enough to help **COW** on
his own.

Luckily **Duck** has an idea – we'll use the
Sandals' long ladder. We fetches it from the
barn and places it against the end of the
house. I has never climbed a ladder before.

"**Just follow me,**" says **Duck**, hopping on to
the first step. "**Ladder-climbing's easy!**"

I slowly follows him, but it doesn't feel
easy at all. Trotters is really not the

best things for
climbing ladders. I
wishes I had flappy
feet like **Duck's**
that would make it
easier to hold on –
although if I did I would look pretty silly.

Every time I moves my trotters, the
ladder wobbles. I steps one way
and the ladder wobbles
that way. I steps
the other way and
it does an even
bigger wobble
that way.

Soon the ladder and me and **Duck** is rocking all over the place. I really doesn't like it!

Finally I reaches the top. I stands on the roof and – aaaaaaaaaaghhhhhh! – I nearly slides straight off. Luckily I manages to catch hold of the ridge bit in the middle with my front trotters. I hangs there wondering what to do next.

"Smart move," says **Duck,** **"sliding along the roof on your belly, Commando Style. I like it!"**

HOORAY! I IS SMART. I is not sure what Commando Style is, but I doesn't tell **Duck** that. I swings my back legs from side to side and pulls myself along the ridge with my front trotters.

Duck is having no problems walking on the roof. He gets to the chimney and reaches down to **COW.** She tries to grab hold of his wing, but she can't quite reach it and instead slips a bit further down the roof.

"NOOOOOOOOOOOOO," she sobs.

"Hang on!" I says. "It's going to be OK." I doesn't know how it's going to be OK though. We has no plan.

And when I finally reaches **COW**, it is really not OK.

I hears a terrible groaning noise. Roofs is used to having little birds on them, not me and **COW**.

As I looks down, the roof under us starts to bend, then...

CRAAAASHHHHHHHH!

"ARRRRGGGGHHH!!!!"

we is falling.

BOOOOOMMFFFF!!!!!

We lands in a big white thing what looks like a large food trough. I lands on top of **COW**, and **DUCK** lands on the top of me. We all looks at each other. What has we done?

Then what we has done gets worse again. There is a big CREEAAAAAK! and a large GROOOOOAAAAAN! and the food trough falls through the floor. BOIIIIING! We lands on something big and bouncy – a **Farmer** bed.

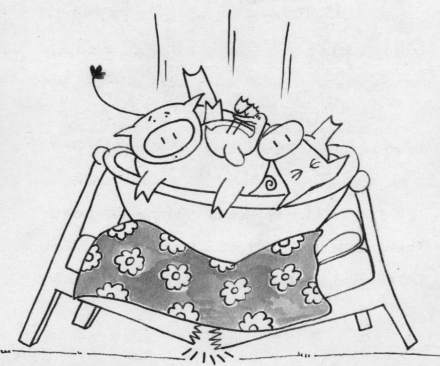

we does a little bounce. But the bed can't take our weight either, and it snaps in two.

Bits of wood flies up around us and we crashes through the floor again.

CRUNCH!!!

we lands in the kitchen on **Mr and Mrs Sandal's** table. We squashes it flat, just as they is having their lunch. **Mrs Sandal's** eyes look like they is about to pop out of her head and **Mr Sandal** is so shocked the carrot he is eating falls out of his mouth on to the floor. I thinks about rushing over and gobbling it up, but I decides this might not be the best moment.

They looks back and forth from us to
the hole we has made through their house.
I looks up; I can see all the way up to the
sky.

This is SUPER-SUPER bad. I doesn't know
what to do, so I scrambles out of the trough

and runs towards the door. **Duck** does the same. I keeps running until I gets to my house, where I buries myself in my straw.

I closes my eyes and tries to pretend that all that didn't just happen, but then I hears this terrible sound coming from the house.

"nooooooooooooooooooooooooo! ohhhhhhh! nooooooooooo!"

It's **COW** – she is still inside. Maybe she got stuck in the trough? I peeks out of my shed just in time to see her come running out of the front door. **Mr Sandal** follows her, shouting and shaking his fist.

As I writes this I is still trembling. The **Sandals** rescued us from the **Old Farmers' Home** and this is how we pays them back, by destroying their house.

Goodsiebadsieday

Hello.

This morning I woke up SUPER early. Normally, this would be because I is excited. But today I is the opposite of excited. I feels awful.

I crawls out of bed and walks over to **Duck Pond**. As I passes **cow shed** I hears **COW** sobbing. I peeks in and she looks up at me. Big tears drips off the end of her nose.

"**woc salt**," she says over and over. "Salt" is a VERY sad word in Pig. If Pigs eats salt they dies. We only says it when things is REALLY bad.

COW follows me over to **Duck Pond**. **Duck** is awake too. We all sits on the side and says nothing. We just stares over at the **Farmer** House. **Mr Sandal** has put a big blue sheet over the hole in the roof.

"What is we going to do to make it up to them?" I asks **Duck**.

He just shrugs and shakes his head. **COW** starts to sob again, and her big tears plop into the pond. I worries the pond will flood if she carries on crying like this.

"We've only just got back into the Sandals' Good Book after our last little adventure," says Duck. **"I am really not sure how we are going to get back in it this time."**

I is not knowing that the **Sandals** has a Good Book! I wonders what is in it, and where they keeps it. I'd love to see it. Perhaps **Duck** could read it to me. Maybe it is like a diary, only with all the bad bits taken out.

I feels terrible, but I knows what will make me feel better – a bite of my enormous organik carrot. I goes back to my shed to dig it up. But when I gets to it, it

looks all sad and
droopy, just like
how I feels. It is
no bigger than
when I planted it.

In fact, I thinks it might actually have
shrunk a bit. I gobbles it up, but it doesn't
make me feel any better. Not even a
teensy bit. I knows things is very wrong
when not even vegytables makes me feel
better.

I is so sad that I lies down and has a
little secret cry.

And because I is lying down, I falls asleep.

I is woken by a loud banging noise. I goes
outside to see what is happening. **Mr Sandal**

is up on the roof, trying to fix it.

Me, **COW** and **Duck** all watches him. The wind is blowing very hard. A really big whoosh of air nearly knocks him off. He has to grab on to the chimney to stop himself being blown away.

"**where's woc?**" says **COW**.

"**COW!**" says **Duck** in a very serious voice. "**I can't believe you want to play the game that got us all in so much trouble.**"

"**no, where's woc?**" **COW** says again in a slightly trembly voice.

We both turns around, thinking maybe she's gone mad. But she hasn't — she's gone blind. A piece of paper covered in **Farmer** writing has blown across her face. I pulls it off and hands it to **Duck**.

He reads out what it says on the paper:

LOCAL COUNTRY SHOW –

CALL FOR ENTRIES.

DO YOU HAVE A PRIZE-

WINNING ANIMAL?

WOULD YOU LIKE TO WIN A FANTASTIC

TROPHY?

WE HAVE CATEGORIES FOR ALL FARM

ANIMALS.

JOIN US THIS SATURDAY ON THE VILLAGE

PLAYING FIELD.

"What's a trophy?" I asks, hoping it is some
kind of really tasty veggie.

32

Duck tells us it's a special thing what looks like a slops bowl with big handles. **Duck** says **Farmers** loves to win them. I guesses it's so they can fill them up with yummy slops; that's what I'd do.

COW'S bottom suddenly starts to wiggle like crazy.

"**woc big parsnip! woc win trophy**."

As she says this she flexes all her big new muscles and swings her enormous udder.

"**I think you might be on to something,**" says Duck. "**We can't fix their roof, but we can make them proud. This could be a great way to get back into their Good Book.**"

I is super happy **Duck** thinks we is going

to be able to get back in the **Sandals'** Good
Book. My bottom is too. It lets
out a massive, happy fart.

"**lion**," says **COW**.

We all starts laughing and **COW'S**
bottom wiggles so hard she nearly falls over.
Somehow I is sure that everything is going
to be OK.

HA! HA! HA!

Horrorday

Hello.

This is a message to me, from me:

PIG, REMEMBER NOT TO BE WRITING THAT
YOU IS SURE EVERYTHING IS GOING TO BE
OK, BECAUSE IT MEANS EVERYTHING IS
NOT GOING TO BE OK. OK?!

Duck tells us that the show is on Saturday
(**Farmer** names is so boring sounding),
and that Saturday is tomorrow. We has no
time to lose!

We spends all day making **COW** look
great. We plays lots of **where's**

WOC? to help make her muscles as big as possible, and **Duck** gives her a wash and polish. I never knew he was so good at washing. **COW** sits in his pond whilst he scrubs her and then buffs her with his feathery bottom. By the end she is almost shining.

Duck says we should leave tonight, in the middle of the night, so the **Sandals** won't see us go. He also says that there won't be any **Farmers** around as they will all be in bed.

So that is what we does.

We meets at the gate when the moon is at the top of the sky. The **Sandals** always locks the gate at night, so we has to squeeze ourselves out through a small hole in the hedge. The small hole is not so small once me and **COW** has been through it.

Next we walks to the Villidge. It is very quiet. Like **Duck** said, all the **Farmers** is asleep.

In the middle of the Villidge is a huge white thing what **Duck** says is called a "tent". This is where the show is going to be. Inside there is lots of pens to keep the animals in, and in the centre there is this special area what **Duck** says is called the "ring", where the competition is going to happen.

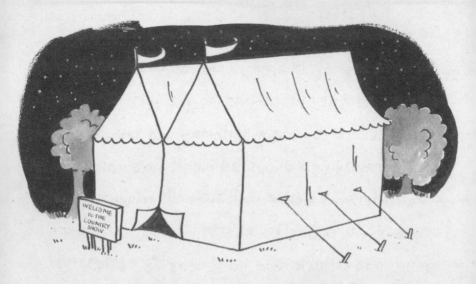

We helps **COW** into one of the pens and then me and **DUCK** hides behind a pile of hay bales in the corner and has a little sleep.

The **Farmers** arrives super early and soon the tent starts to fill up. Everyone is so busy that no one notices **COW**.

COW'S competition is second, after the

Turkey one. **Turkeys** is very, very strange-looking birds. They is super feathery and their heads looks like they has melted a bit on a hot day — I has drawn a picture so you can sees what I means.

There is this one **Turkey** in particular what is very funny. All the other **Turkeys** just walk around the pen bobbing their ugly heads up and down and ruffling their feathers. But this one goes crazy. First of all he doesn't walk around the ring, he struts up and down the middle, and every time he turns he does these huge spins and swooshes his massive

tail around. Finally he struts to the edge
of the ring, does a double spin, and takes a
bow in front of this SUPER-UGLY LADY FARMER.

She is the most UGLY FARMER I has
ever seen. The skin on her
face looks like there is not
enough of it. It's stretched
super tight. And it's a
very strange orange colour.
I has never seen an orange
Farmer. She has teeny-tiny lips. They
is twisted into a shape what looks like
she has just eaten something very sour. I
can't see her eyes 'cos she is wearing these
things what **Duck** says is called "sunglasses".
Strange, I thinks, there is no sun in here!

She wears a long black coat what goes all the way to the floor. I doesn't like the look of her.

The mad **Turkey** wins a trophy and everyone claps and smiles.

Then the cow competition starts. There is five in the competition; they is all super shiny and muscly like **COW** and has big udders too. I crosses all my trotters. I notices that **Duck** has crossed his flippery feet.

The first cow walks into the ring. She is black and she trots around like a horse, which seems to impress all the **Farmers**. They all cheers as the black cow trots around one way, then the other. Finally, she trots over to a **Farmer** who inspects her udders and milks her. The black cow has lots of milk.

I imagines myself being the one what is doing the milking. What an AMAZING job that would be. When no one was looking I could squirt some of the milk into my mouth. Mmmmmm, I thinks. Yummy, yummy! **Duck** gives me a nudge and I realizes that I is saying "Mmmmmmm" out loud. Whoopsie.

The next three cows is all good too. There is a big brown one what can swish her tail round and round in circles, a white one with enormous muscles, and one with super-long hair and twirly-whirly horns. They is all good at milk-making. I feels very thirsty.

Finally it's **COW'S** turn. I can tell she is nervous because she keeps blinking. **COW** has very long eyelashes, so it's easy to spot.

As **COW** walks into the ring I notices the crazy **Turkey**, who is standing with his trophy next to the SUPER-UGLY FARMER, start pointing his wing at her and making excited **Turkey** noises. He clearly thinks **COW** looks good — maybe he's not quite as bonkers after all. The SUPER-UGLY FARMER stares at him. I guesses she doesn't like how noisy he is being. The **Turkey** gets even more excited and does even more pointing. THE SUPER-UGLY FARMER

looks over at **COW** and rubs her hands
together like she's cold – that's strange,
I thinks. She is wearing such a big
coat. She really is a very odd
Farmer.

COW'S walk is great. She
looks amazing. I is so proud of her.

Finally, she walks over to
where the milking **Farmer**
with the bucket is. The
Farmer places the bucket
under **COW'S** enormous udder.
She looks very impressed.
I is not surprised. I thinks
COW must have been making
extra special amounts of milk

especially for this moment; her udder's twice as big as my head. The **Farmer** reaches up and starts to milk ...

... but nothing comes out ...

... not even a drop.

The tent goes silent. The milking **Farmer** tries again, a little harder.

Come on, **COW**, I thinks.

I looks at **COW'S** face. A tiny tear trickles down her cheek and plops into the straw. I suddenly realizes **COW'S** problem; she is too nervous to make any milk!

I starts to panic. I doesn't know what to do or how to help, but, luckily, my bottom does! It lets out the most enormous, creaky-sounding fart. FRIB-BERRRRRT!

"**frog!**" says **cow**, and bursts out laughing. The laughing makes her relax and milk suddenly shoots out at top speed. It fills the bucket in seconds. It comes out so fast that the milking **Farmer** simply can't control control her udders; they is wiggling round like crazy fingers. Milk fires

everywhere, covering all the **Farmers** what is watching. I has never seen so much milk in all my life. I don't think the **Farmers** has either.

By the time **COW'S** udders is empty, everything is soaked. There is even milk dripping from the roof of the tent.

For a moment everyone goes super quiet. All I can hear is the drip, drip, drip of **COW'S** milk.

But then, suddenly —

"**RAAAARRRRRR!**" – all the **Farmers** starts to cheer and clap.

COW looks very pleased with herself.

All the other cows is brought back in and lined up next to her. I can tell they is jealous.

A big **Farmer** in a long white coat comes in. In his hand he holds an enormous silver slops bowl, with twirly-whirly handles — the trophy! He walks up and down the cows, looking at them carefully.

I holds my breath. Please let **COW** win. Please, please.

The big **Farmer** takes the trophy and ... PLACES IT IN FRONT OF **COW**!!!!!!

BEST IN SHOW — COW

SHE'S WON!!!!!!!!!

Duck and I gives each other big "well done" pats on the back. Mine is a little bit hard and nearly knocks him over, I is soooooo excited. **COW** looks really happy; her bottom is doing massive wiggles.

The big **Farmer** says something into a magic stick that makes his voice very loud.

"They're asking for her owner to come and collect her and the trophy," says **Duck**.

All the **Farmers** looks around to see who **COW** belongs to. But of course the **Sandals** is not here.

"What shall we do?" I whispers to **Duck**.

But before **Duck** has time to answer, the SUPER- UGLY FARMER struts into the ring. She is wearing the strangest wellie boots I has ever seen. They is very pointy and has these huge heels what makes her very tall. Her long black coat swishes from side to side as she walks.

She comes up to **COW** and runs her hand

along her back. She is wearing black gloves
what makes her hands look like nasty spiders.

Duck and I looks at each other. What is
she doing?? She is not **COW'S** owner!!!

She looks around the ring and does a
twisted little smile what doesn't look real.
All the **Farmers** lets out a gasp –
maybe they knows her? She
stops smiling and pulls a

rope out of one of her coat pockets. She ties it around **COW'S** neck, gives it a hard yank and struts back out of the ring pulling **COW** behind her!

Duck and I quickly sneaks out of the tent to see where the SUPER-UGLY FARMER is taking her. But we can't see either of them. Where has they gone? Before I has a chance to ask I hears a noise.

WUMP! WUMP! WUMP!

All the straw around us blows up and swirls around. It whips my face and makes it sting. I closes my eyes for a second and when I opens them I sees a terrible sight.

Lifting up into the air above the tent is a strange-looking flying machine. It looks

a bit like a tractor if you took the wheels
off, put a big
glass bubble on
the front and two
spinning sticks on top.

Underneath,
something large and
black-and-white is
hanging in a huge net.

IT'S **COW**!!!!

COW is being
lifted up in the air. Up,
up, up she goes. Then WUMP! WUMP! WUMP!
the whirling Bubble Tractor turns and
flies away.

"**COW**!!!!" I screams. "COME BACK!!!!!!!!!!!!"

I starts to run after her but, as I is looking up in the sky and not where I is going, I runs straight into the crazy **Turkey**. I knocks him to the floor.

"**Gub, gib, gob, gab!**" he blurts out in an odd-sounding voice.

"What do you mean?" I says, not understanding his funny **Turkey** words. "What has happened to **COW**? Where is she going?"

"**Where is she going?**" says the **Turkey**, now speaking in Pig but with a strange, high-pitched voice. "**Only to the most wonderful place in the whole wide world!**"

I has a horrible feeling he is lying.

Time Till Cow Is A Handbag: Two Days!

I NO LONGER CARES ABOUT THE GOOD BOOK AND THE **Sandals'** ROOF BECAUSE **COW** HAS BEEN KIDNAPPED!!! AND WE ONLY HAS TWO DAYS TO SAVE HER FROM BEING TURNED INTO A HANDBAG!!!!!!!!!!!!!!!!!

We finds all this out from the crazy **Turkey**.

"Who is you?" I asks, getting up off him. "What is you talking about?"

The **Turkey** brushes the dust off his feathers.

"**Well, I am Ki-Ki,**" he says, waving his wing at himself. "**I dropped the 'Turk' bit of my name – so boring, don't you think? My star sign is Capricorn, and I'm into fashion, beauty, skincare and nail art. How about you, you look like a ... hmmm ... Pisces? No, no, wait a minute, a Leo.**"

"I is a Pig," I says, "and I doesn't have time to answer your strange questions – I wants to know what happened to **COW!!**"

"**OK! OK! Cool your trotters! You really have no reason to worry. She's being looked after by the wonderful** IVANNA HERTCHEW. **You must have heard of her! She's one of the richest, most** famous people in all the world. And don't tell me you haven't heard about her incredible handbag collection – it's a wonder to behold! She has every handbag ever made. And now, she has started to make her own handbags – and your lucky friend is going to be made into one!!!!"

"A handbag?" I says.

"**Yes, yes, indeed!**" says **Ki-Ki**, clapping his wings together. "**And if she's very lucky, maybe a matching purse too!**"

I thinks from the look on my face that **Ki-Ki** can tell I has no idea what he is talking about.

"**A handbag!**" he says excitedly, pointing

at a large sack what is hanging
on a lady **Farmer's** arm.
"I mean IVANNA'S are much
more beautiful than that old
thing, but you get the idea.
Wouldn't you like to be one?
Surely it's everyone's dream? To be an
original IVANNA HERTCHEW handbag – how
glorious!"

Duck and I both stares at **Ki-Ki**. He is
even madder than the crazy frogs what
hop around in **Duck Pond**.

"No!" I says. "I doesn't want to be
anything else but myself. I doesn't want
to die!!"

"Oh, no," says **Ki-Ki**, "you don't die!

I mean, yes, you do in one sense. But
as a handbag – a piece of IVANNA'S art
– you live on FOR EVER. You'll be
placed alongside the most beautiful
bags ever made! There isn't possibly a
better compliment!!!"

"All right," says Duck, "so where does this
IVANNA HERTCHEW live?"

"So you DO want to be a handbag,
I knew it! IVANNA lives in MAISON MORBEEDE,
of course. It's on the Other Side, over
the Sea. If you want to be a bag this
week, you're going to need to get
there super fast. IVANNA has a motto –
'Mince them on Monday, tan them on
Tuesday'. By Wednesday you and your

58

friend the **COW** could be sitting side by side on IVANNA'S shelf, covered in diamonds and buckles!"

"We DON'T want to be handbags! We want to save our friend!" says **Duck** firmly.

"Well, you simply don't know what you're missing," says **Ki-Ki**, happily admiring his odd-looking toenails.

Duck tells me the sea is like the biggest **Duck Pond** I has ever seen. The Other Side, he says, is just like here — only the **Farmers** talks a bit funny.

"The problem is," he says, looking worried, "I have never been that far." He thinks for a moment and then turns to **Ki-Ki**. "How about you show us the way? If you help us find **COW**, we'll let you come with us! You can meet your 'wonderful' IVANNA."

"Are you serious? Me go to MAISON MORBEEDE? Yes! Just imagine what an exquisite, feathery bag I would make!" He does a twirl in front of us. "I'm thinking something sparkly, with a glitter finish and star-shaped buttons. What do you think?"

Me and **Duck** looks at each other. I doesn't know quite what to say and neither, it seems, does he.

"All right, I hear you!" says **Ki-Ki**. "Maybe star-shaped buttons are a step too far. How about diamond ones?"

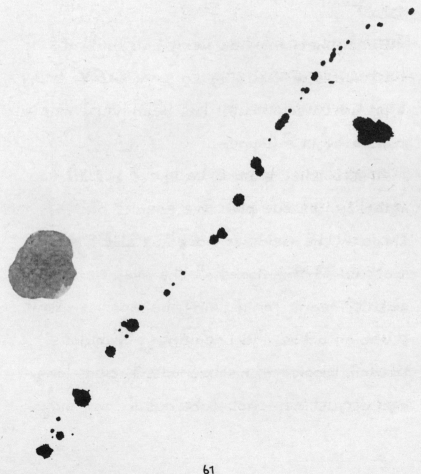

Time Till Cow Is A Handbag: Two Days Minus A Bit!!

Hello.

Everything may be very bad, but at least we is on our way to save **COW**. And I is proud to say that I has been very helpful in making this happen.

First we heads back to the **Farm** to make our rescue plan. We sneaks back through the fields so no **Farmer** will spot us. **Ki-Ki** moans all the way. He says he wasn't meant for walking; he worries about stubbing a toe and breaking a "fabulous" toenail. I looks at his toenails. They is long and disgusting — not fabulous in any way.

I asks **Ki-Ki** who his owner is. "Won't they be worried you is missing?" I asks.

"**I don't have an owner,**" he says proudly.

"**So, you're wild?**" says **Duck**.

"**Well, you could say I have a wild streak,**" says **Ki-Ki**, doing one of his silly twirls, "**but I prefer the term 'free-range'. Fantastically free-range!**"

"**That would explain why you speak Pig so well,**" says **Duck**.

He explains that wild animals speaks everyone's languages. That way, wherever they goes, they can always have a chat. **Duck** says his mother was a wild **Duck** what came

yuck!

to live on **Duck Pond**. She taught him all the languages she knew. I can't believe he has not told me this before. All this time I has been thinking that he is just super clever!

Finally we reaches my house. We huddles together inside.

"**Right,**" **Duck** whispers, tapping his head with his wing, "**how are we going to get to MAISON MORBEEDE?**"

Ki-Ki starts doing some over-the-top umm-ing and ahh-ing.

I stares out, hoping an idea is going to pop into my head. But all that pops into my head is turnips. A big box of turnips. I can sees it sitting with all the other boxes of delicious veggies, packed up and written on, ready to be collected. Get out of my head, turnips, I thinks. You is teasing me. You will never be mine. Soon the lorry is going to come and take you away and deliver you to **Farmers** over the world... All over the world... ALL OVER THE WORLD!

"I has got it," I says. "We can send ourselves to MAISON MORBEEDE in one of **Mr and Mrs Sandal's** special veggie boxes! We just need to find one what goes to the Other side."

"**Wow!**" says **Duck**. "**Pig, that is maybe the best idea you have ever had.**"

My tummy does a little happy loop-the-loop.

"**Your best idea?**" says **Ki-Ki**. "Are

you pulling my leg? I am a prize-winning Turkey; I don't do 'being packed into boxes'!"

I looks at **Ki-Ki's** leg. It is short and scaly. And I isn't anywhere near it. What a funny thing to say!

"If you doesn't want to come," I says, "I is sure we will be fine without you."

"**Oh, no! No! No!**" says **Ki-Ki**, looking a little panicked. "**Only joking. I love going in boxes really — look how excited this face is!**"

It's hard to see what his face is, 'cos it is mostly covered in long dangly red bits.

I sees **Mr and Mrs Sandal** getting their special bicycle out of the shed. **Mr Sandal** does the pedalling while **Mrs Sandal** sits in the box on the front calling **COW'S** name. They must be realizing she is missing. They cycles off out of the gate. I feels sad – they is never going to find her.

We goes over to the boxes and **Duck** starts reading out the labels to **Ki-Ki**. I has never heard of any of the places – they all sounds very strange to me: Germ-any, Eye-land, Gnaw-way. **"Nope,"** says **Ki-Ki**, shaking his head at each place. **"Uh-uh, no,** sireee." **Duck** gets down to the last two: a big one and a not-so-big one. He reads the label on the largest first: "**Bell-jam**."

"**N-O spells no!**" says **Ki-Ki**, who seems to be really enjoying this game.

Duck reads the final one: Fraanz.

"**Nnnn — yes!**" **Kiki** says, looking a little surprised then a lot worried when sees the size of the box. It's going to be a squeeze to get us all in.

YES! We has found a box what is going to get us to **COW**!!!

Duck opens the lid. It's full of delicious cabbyages.

"Don't worry," I says, "I'll make some room!" and I takes a big bite out of one.

Oh, boy! Organik cabbyages
tastes AMAZING, AMAZING,
AMAZING! I can't believe
I is getting to eat a
whole box full. This
is like my veggie
dream come true.

"**I've heard cabbage does incredible
things for your skin**," says **Ki-Ki**,
patting his face with his wing.

"Really?" I says. "All I knows they is
good for is this," and I lets out a little
cabbyagy fart.

"**OMG!**" says **Ki-Ki**, staggering backwards.
"**That's the worst...**" and then he falls
down dead. My fart has killed **Ki-Ki**!

Duck waddles over and puts his head next to **Ki-Ki's**.

"**Don't worry, he's still breathing,**" he says. "**Your fart just knocked him out.**"

Phew! Organik cabbyage farts is super powerful.

Duck fetches my water bowl and pours it over **Ki-Ki's** head.

"**Please tell me I've died and come back as a feathered clutch,**" he says, spluttering back to life.

"Nope!" I says: "You is still you. My super-stinky fart knocked you out. Sorry."

"**Oh, what a shame,**" says **Ki-Ki**, looking rather upset.

We squeezes ourselves into the box: me

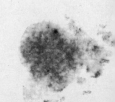

on the bottom and **Ki-Ki** and **Duck** on my back. **Ki-Ki** makes me promise that I won't do another "**total and utter mind-bending stinker**". I agrees I won't, but secretly I crosses my trotters.

I will write again soon. For now I has to be quiet and still so the **Farmer** what collects the boxes doesn't discover us.

Time Till Cow Is A Handbag: One Day And A Half!!!

Hello.

We isn't having to wait long for the lorry to come and collect us. I hears it pull up, then some **Farmer** voices talking, and then finally I feels our box being lifted up. I hears the lorry engine start up and we moves off. Hooray! My idea worked. I feels very proud.

There is a little hole in the side of the box what I can just see out of, but in the back of the lorry all I can see is black. This is super boring, so I soon falls asleep, dreaming of more organik cabbyages.

I is just having a dream where I is tucking into one what is as big as **Duck**, when I is woken by a loud bang. I looks out through my looking hole. The back of the truck opens. This must be the Other Side – we has made it!!!

A **Farmer** dressed all in blue with a pointy hat shines a torch into the back of the lorry. I describes him to **Duck**.

"**Uh-oh! It's the Police,**" he says. He tells me the **Police** is a special sort of **Farmer** what locks you up if you has done something bad. He whispers that he thinks we must be at something called a Port. This isn't the Other Side; this is a place you goes to get across the sea to get there. He says the **Police** has to check the boxes to make sure there is nothing bad inside them.

"But we is inside them," I whispers. "What if they finds us? They'll lock us up and we'll never get to **COW!**"

I starts to panic. All the organik cabbyages in my tummy starts to grumble and rumble.

"No!" whispers **Ki-Ki**, **"You promised."**

I squeezes my bottom together. Now would be a REALLY bad time to let out a big fart. Mouse, I thinks — tiny fart, tiny fart, just a little "eeeeek, eeeeeeek". But then, HOOOONK! I does a big, stinky Goose fart.

"OM..." says **Ki-Ki**, and then I feels him

go all floppy on my back. I has knocked him out again.

I peers through my spy hole. I can't see the **Police**. Phew! I thinks maybe he has gone away. But he hasn't. "**EURGHHHH!**" I hears him shout. I knows what that means: my enormous, stinking, organik fart has hit his nose.

"Oh no," says **Duck**, "**he thinks he can smell a rotten batch of veggies**."

Before I has time to panic even more, the lid of our box opens and the **Police** is staring down at us. **Duck** pecks him on the nose and he falls backwards holding his face.

We quickly scrambles out. **Ki-Ki** is still passed out, so I grabs him in my mouth as

gently as I can. We clambers
out of the back of the
lorry and on to the ground.
It's night-time, but there
is lots of lights on tall
sticks, what makes it
seem like daytime.

Lined up around us
is other lorries. More
of the **Police**
comes running
towards us – they
has big sticks
in their hands.
Me and **Duck** runs
from under one lorry

to the next until the lorries runs out and we is left on the edge of this flat, black land. I hears the **Police** voices behind us get closer and closer.

"The street light in the corner of the car park is broken." **Duck** points at a tall stick what has no light at the top of it. **"Run for that and hopefully we will be able to lose the Police in the dark."**

I does the fastest run I can. The funny, wobbly red bits on **Ki-Ki's** face slaps against my cheeks, and his feathers tickles my nose.

We runs into the corner of the car park and keeps going. The **Police** voices starts to fade. Animals is good at seeing in the

dark, but **Police** and **Farmers** is
not. We keeps on running until we can't
hear them any more. The tickling finally
gets too much and I does a big sneeze.
Ki-Ki flies out of my mouth and lands on
the ground in front of us.

"**Tell me I'm an oversized handbag
with a feather fringe, tassels and
and a velvet lining,**" he says, running his
wings over his body.

"Nope, sorry," I says, "I knocked you out
with my fart again. But the good news is, I
saved you from the **Police.**"

"**Really?**" says **Ki-Ki**, looking confused,
"**You saved me????**"

"Yes!" I says, wondering if my fart has

made him go a bit deaf.

"No one has ever done anything nice for me," he says, and his eyes starts to water. **"No one, ever..."**

I feels a bit awkward about this, so I quickly changes what we is talking about. "What's that noise?" I asks. I can hear a loud swishing: swish, it goes, then swooosh.

"It's the Sea," says **Duck**. **"We're on a beach – that's what all this sand is."**

I looks down. My trotters is sunk into this strange yellow stuff; I guesses this is what he means by sand. It seems a bit silly to me – there is no way you could roll around and have a bath in it like you can with mud.

Stuck in the sand is these small white things **Ki-Ki** says is called "shells". He runs around collecting them to make himself what he calls a "**spectacular necklace**".

I walks towards the swishy noise. I can't wait to see this enormous **Duck Pond**. I gets to the edge of it — it is more enormous than enormous. It sparkles under the light of the twinkly stars. I thought I would be able to see MAISON MORBEEDE, but I can't see anything but water and more water.

"How is we going to get across it? It's so big!" I shouts back at the others.

"**I'm not sure,**" says **Duck**, shaking his head. He sits down next to me and lets out a long sigh. I knows he won't say this, but it's

all my fault we got found by the **Police**
and is now looking at the sea rather than
going across it to rescue **COW**.

I sits down next to him. I feels more
terrible than terrible. My bottom and me
has totally messed up.

The sun starts to come up and this
makes the sea look even bigger.

If we doesn't reach **COW** I is never
forgiving myself.

Time Till Cow Is A Handbag: Just One Day!!!!

Hello.

If you ever tried to make up something as bonkers as what happened to us next, you would never be able to.

It all started with a loud CLANK! and a big BANG!

Soon after the sun comes up we hears these loud noises coming from behind a big rock further along the beach. The banging and clanking gets louder and faster.

Duck signals with his wing for us to follow him. We gets to the rock and peers around it. Behind it is the strangest thing what I

has ever seen. It's ginormous and looks like a huge metal poo, with a little metal shed on top. And, hitting it with a hammer, is an animal what also looks a bit like a poo, with flappy feet and a funny tail.

"Wow! What's that?" I whispers. But I is guessing my whisper is not that quiet, as the poo shouts back in funny-sounding Pig.

"*Ahoy there, Pig, old boy, have you never set eyes on a Seal before? I am The Captain. Now how about you all come over and tell me what, in the name of Neptune, you are doing on my beach?*"

Ki-Ki prances out

from behind the rock. I
thinks he is trying to
show off.

"**Well, I'm Ki-Ki**,"
he sings, dancing up to
The Captain and shaking his tail
feathers in his face. "**And can I just say
you have the most beautifully smooth
skin. You must exfoliate daily!**"

"*Erm, well, I, err...*" says *The Captain*,
looking slightly embarrassed.

Duck ignores **Ki-Ki's** crazy dancing and
fills *The Captain* in about **COW** and IVANNA
HERTCHEW.

"*Well, well,*" he says, stroking his long,
white whiskers with one of his flappy feet,

"we can't let the evil harpy harm your dear friend now, can we?"

He gives the rusty, metal poo-shaped thing another bang with his hammer. "If only Old Celia here was in working order, I'd whisk you over to the Other Side myself."

"Old Celia?" I says.

"Ah, of course you landlubbers won't have seen a submarine before. This is a 1914 'C' class sub. She washed up here a year or two ago. I've been restoring her ever since. One day, my Old Celia shall power through the water again, like an ocean-going Cheetah."

"Old Celia goes in the water? Surely she just sinks!" I says. I sinks in water and I is a lot lighter than the submarine.

"Yes, my porcine friend — she goes under the water," says The Captain proudly. "Think of her like an underwater tractor, if that helps you understand."

Old Celia is the strangest-looking tractor what I has ever seen. But then The Captain is the strangest-looking animal. They goes well together.

"Now, Old Celia might not be able to take you, but I know a likely bunch who will. Come, my lovelies, follow me," he says, and he flops off up the beach. *Seals* is moving very strangely. I is so happy that I has legs not flippers.

We follows *The Captain* towards some huge rocks.

"*Ahoy there,*" shouts *The Captain* at the top of his voice.

From out of the rocks flies a flock of **Gulls**. They swoops down and lands in front of us. I has only ever seen **Gulls** from a distance. When the **Farmer** across the valley ploughs his field they comes to look for worms. They is quite a bit bigger close up – they must eat A LOT of worms.

"*Comrades,*" says *The Captain*, "*may I present to you my new friends, Pig,* **Duck** *and, er,* **Ki-Ki**."

Me and **Duck** does a little wave and **Ki-Ki** does a twirl, showing off his "spectacular necklace".

"**Oi! Oi! Saveloy,**" says one of the **Gulls**,

stepping forwards. "Pleased ta meecha. I'm the Beakanator and these muckers here is my boyz." He flicks his wing at the bunch of Gulls stood behind him. "Sir Flap-a-Lot, McSquawkster, the Hop Meister, Wingo Star and Tiny."

Duck was right about all wild animals talking Pig, but The Beakanator talks a kind of Pig what is super hard for even me to understand — and I is a Pig.

"A terrible tragedy has befallen their bovine buddy the **COW**. *The poor lady has been kidnapped,"* continues *The Captain.*

"Flippin' Nora!" says The Beakanator. "Someone's tea-leafed a **COW**."

"Yes, the evil harpy IVANNA HERTCHEW *has thieved the* **COW**. *My friends must get to the Other*

Side before she is turned into a handbag," says *The Captain,* who clearly has no trouble understanding him.

"Well, me old chinas," says The Beakanator, "we'd be 'appy to 'elp. A friend in need is a friend indeed an' all. We goes over the Other Side all the time. They've got top grub over there, ain't they? Them foreign types knows how to cook."

"But you can fly," I says. "I can't."

"Fly? Us? You must be havin' a larf," says The Beakantor.

"Haw! Haw! Haw!" laughs all the Gulls.

"Nah, me old Piggy mucker, we ain't wearin' ourselves out wiv that flying malarkey. We takes the boat. It goes over twice a day, dunnit?"

"A boat?" I asks.

The Beakanator points his wing at this little white thing what is bobbing up and down on the Sea. It looks tiny. There is no way we is all going to fit on it.

"Well, technically speakin', it's a ferry. It takes numpties – I fink you calls 'em **Farmers** – across the Sea. And I knows what you're finkin': it looks dinky – but believe you me, up close it's massif."

"And not only that," says the one what I think is called Sir Flap-a-Lot, "it's got I-screams onit."

The mention of I-screams makes all the Gulls

very excited. I is not sure why — I-screams sounds scary!

I is just about to ask what they is when The Captain says, "It's perfect, but just one problem: they won't notice a **Duck** on board, what with him being a bird of the water variety and all, but Pig and **Ki-Ki** will stand out like a sore flipper."

"No problemo, guvnor. You leave that to us, we'll sort 'em right out, won't we, boyz?" says The Beakanator, rubbing his wings together. "Now, come this way, gentlemen, if you purlease." He leads us over to the bottom of the big rocks. All over the beach there

is huge white blobs of Gull poo and feathers.
Ki-Ki makes a noise like he is going to be
sick.

"Now what you two is needing," says The
Beakanator, "is one blindin' disguise. 'Specially you,
Pigster. And what betta way to disguise you, than to
turn you into someone like Tiny here?"

He points his wing to the biggest,
featheriest Gull of all. I has no idea why
they calls him Tiny. He's huge.

"Genius, bruv," says Tiny.
"Let's cover 'em all in
feathers; the **Turkey**
won't need many, but the
Pigster'll need the full monty."

"Haw! Haw! Haw!"

Tiny??

The Gulls all finds this idea hilarious.

"And we can glue 'em on wiv this," he says, scooping up some of the white poo and walking towards us.

"**Woah there!**" squawks **Ki-Ki**. "**If you think you're putting that on me, you can think again! I am not going to turn myself into a mobile muck heap!**"

"Suit yourself, Keekster," says The Beakanator, "but we ain't gonna be responsible if some numpty spots ya and turns ya inta a Christmas dinna, is we, boyz?"

Ki-Ki mumbles something about his name not being Keekster and says he will find a better disguise. But I has no choice. I lets the Gulls get to work. First they covers me in a layer of Gull poo. This is not the first time I has been covered in poo. The last poo I was covered in was very heavy. Gull poo is nice and light, which is great. But it does smell quite strongly of fish, which is not so great.

Once 1 is totally covered they starts sticking on feathers.

Duck sits on a rock and watches. He is so lucky that he has feathers of his own. The **Gulls** is very fast, and soon 1 is covered from head to toe. They makes me a beak using some large shells and straps them on to my face with this slimy green stuff called seaweed.

I looks down at myself. I makes a great Gull. A Pigull. Ha! Ha! I is still very funny, even when I is in disguise.

"**Ta-dah!**" says **Ki-Ki**, twirling out from behind a rock. Instead of covering himself in feathers, **Ki-Ki** has made an enormous feathery hat, what he has tied on top of his head with some old rope.

"Blimey, Keekster," says The Beakanator. "Anyone would fink you was off to see the Kween."

"**I call it the Fabulous Fandango,**" says **Ki-Ki**. "**I wouldn't expect birds like you to understand beauty like this.**"

The Gulls all falls about laughing. This makes **Ki-Ki** even crosser. I wants to laugh too, but I can't 'cos I worries my beak will drop off.

The Captain comes over to see what the Gulls has done. **Ki-Ki** rushes over to him and shows off his hat.

"Erm, well, my dear," he says, clearing his throat, *"you really have surpassed yourself."* **Ki-Ki** claps his wings happily.

The Captain looks me up and down. *"And you, my good man, well ... what can I say?"*

"I know," I says, "I looks AMAZING, doesn't I!"

"That's one word for it," he says.

Hooray! *The Captain* thinks I looks great too.

The Beakanator says the ferry leaves soon, so we says goodbye and thank you to *The Captain*. **Ki-Ki** blows him a kiss.

"*Er, thank you, m'dear,*" he says, coughing nervously. "*Bon voyage! As they say.*"

This time, I promises you, I is going to make sure my feathery bottom doesn't do anything bad.

Time Till Cow Is A Handbag: Less Than A Day!!!!!

Hello.

The Beakanator is right. The ferry is much bigger than it looked when it was far off. I has never seen anything like it.

The **Gulls** forms a circle around me and **Ki-Ki** to make it hard for the **Farmers**

to spot us. Gulls doesn't walk; they hops —
so we all hops with them. Hop, hop, hop, we
goes, up the steps from the beach and on
to the enormous wall. I is just like a Gull.
Duck waddles behind.

The closer we gets to the ferry, the
faster my heart starts beating. This might
be because of all the hopping, but I think
it's really because I is super worried that
we might get caught. We doesn't have time
for bad stuff like that to happen.

On the back of the ferry is a large flap
what folds down so the **Farmers** can
get on. We waits until they is all on board
and then we hops on too. I has to admit, my
hop sounds much louder than everyone else's.

Luckily it is not very sunny, so all the **Farmers** goes inside. Phew! We can sits outside and have a little rest.

We all goes up near the pointy bit at the front of the ferry. The Gulls hops up and stands along the bars what runs down the sides. I is too big to hop up beside them, so I just sits on the floor with **Duck** and **Ki-Ki** Ki-Ki complains he feels seasick before the boat has even moved.

I doesn't feel seasick. I feels sea-excited. Being on a boat is great fun. Whoosh! We goes through the water – this must be what it is like being a **Duck**. Sometimes water splashes up, but thanks to my feathers, I doesn't get wet.

Then a family of **Farmers** comes out to look at the sea. The **Mr and Mrs Farmer** puts their arms around each other and stands at the very front. The two **mini-Farmers** is holding these strange cone things with white stuff on top. One of them shouts to the other and they runs towards us, flapping their arms.

"Oi! Oi!" shouts The Beakanator. "Mini-Numpty alert! I-screams at ten o'clock. Assume first positions."

The Gulls all flies up into the air, leaving me, **Duck** and **Ki-Ki** on the floor.

The **mini-Farmers** stops and stares at us. I guesses they has never see a Gull as big as me.

I decides to do my best **Gull** impression. "Squawk," I says. "Squawk, squawk." But this just makes the **mini-Farmers** start laughing. One says something to the other and she reaches out and plucks one of my feathers. They laughs again, and pulls out more feathers.

SQUAWK! SQUAWK!

Duck tries to bite the **mini-Farmer's** bottom, but she moves out of the way just in time.

She waves my feathers in the air and shouts over to the **Mr and Mrs Farmer**, so they can see what she has done.

But her shouts is drowned out by The Beakanator. "I-SCREAMS AWAY! LET'S BE HAVIN' 'EM, BOYZ!"

Whoosh! The Gulls swoops down and plucks the cones out of the **mini-Farmer's** hands. The **mini-Farmers** bursts into tears. They runs back to the **Mr**

and Mrs Farmer and points over to us. The Gulls quickly flock around so we can't be seen.

"Blindin' Cornetto," says Tiny as he tucks into the white stuff what has fallen on to the floor. Gulls seems to be loving their food as much as Pigs!

The **Mr and Mrs Farmer** looks over, but I guesses all they can see is the Gulls eating, 'cos they just gives them an evil stare, puts their arms around the **mini-Farmers** and takes them back inside.

Ha! Ha! **mini-Farmers**, you is not going to pluck me!!!!

The Gulls offers me some of their I-screams. I has a little lick. They is not scary; they is DELICIOUS! Like **COW'S** milk, only much colder. Suddenly I feels guilty for having fun whilst **COW** is in so much trouble. Oh, **COW**, I thinks. We is coming to save you as fast as we can.

As I writes this, I thinks I can spy the Other Side. It's getting closer and closer. I wonders what it will be like, and if they will have any slops. I is starting to feel a bit hungry — I-scream is not really very filling.

Time Till Cow Is A Handbag: Even Less Than Even Less Than One Day!!!!

Hello.

We has made it to the Other Side! I has to admit, I is a little disappointed. It's just the same as where we came from. The trees look the same. The beach looks the same. Even the grass is the same colour. The only thing what is different is that there is a villidge at the

top of the beach instead of big rocks.

Ki-Ki points to a large hill and says that MAISON MORBEEDE is on the Other side of it.

The gulls gathers around us as we hops off the boat. They says they knows a special short-cut road through the villidge, where **Farmers** hardly ever goes.

I soon realizes why they calls it special — the road is full of huge bins what The Beakanator says is for local restaurants. I has no idea what restaurants is, but I guesses they must be places where **Farmers** who don't eat much go, as I spies delicious-looking veggies spilling out of the top of every bin.

I has to say, slops on this side is not smelling like slops back home. The Beakanator says this is because **Farmers** over here covers everything in garlik. I has no idea what this is, but it smells yummy. I so wishes we could stop and have a little nibble, but I knows we doesn't have time for that. My Piggy tummy does a loud rumble, but I tells it to shhhhhhh!

We gets to the bottom of the big hill and the Gulls kindly plucks the feathers off me, and I does a little roll around in the grass to get the dried poo off. **Ki-Ki** huffily agrees to take off the hat, but he says there is N-O way he is going to lose the necklace.

I thanks the Gulls very much for all their help.

"Ah, bee'ayve yourself, you is like a bruver from another muver," says The Beakanator. I think he means that we is related, but I is not sure. Maybe he's forgotten I is a Pig, not a Gull.

"You take care of yourselves now," he says, waving us off up the hill. "I'm sure you'll have no problem sorting out that nasty old Mrs Whats-Her-Knickers."

I would give all the garliky slops in every bin in the world for him to be right.

Time Till Cow Is A Handbag: Nearly No Time!!!!!!!

Hello.

There is no hill I wouldn't climb to get to **COW**. I doesn't care how much my legs hurts, 'cos I knows that if we don't get to her soon, **COW** will be in pain a hundred times worse.

"There it is!" shouts **Ki-Ki** as we reaches the top.

"That's MAISON MARBEEDE!"
I looks at where he is pointing. Down the hill, across a large yellow field, is

a huge house made mostly of black glass. The sun bounces off it; it shines like **Farmer's** tractor did the day he bought it. For a moment I thinks it almost looks sort of nice, but then the wind blows and I smells something horrible.

It smells just like the inside of the shed where **Farmer** was going to chip-chop me up. I starts to panic; I escaped **Farmer**, but what if **COW** can't escape IVANNA? I imagines her being sliced up into handbag shapes and my legs goes a bit wobbly. I tries to pretend it is 'cos they is tired, but I thinks **Duck** knows the real reason. He gives me a look what says, **"It's OK."**

I has to say, I is really not sure it is!!!!!

Luckily, the yummy sweetcorns
in the the yellow field makes me
feel a bit better. I has never
had a sweetcorn before. They
is so delicious, they has just
knocked potato out of the
number two spot on my "most
tasty veggie" list.

yummy
sweetcorns

**"So how are we going to get inside Maison
Morbeede?"** asks **Duck.** "𝕀𝕍𝔸ℕℕ𝔸 **is not just
going to let us in.**"

"How about I eats lots of these yummy
sweetcorns," I suggests, "and then
sees if I can knock her out with
one of my super-stinking farts? It
worked on **Ki-Ki**! Ha! Ha!"

"**That is so NOT funny!**" says **Ki-Ki**
huffily.

Duck says we can't guarantee IVANNA will
be as sensitive as **Ki-Ki**. My farts has
never knocked out a **Farmer** before.

"**I know,**" says **Ki-Ki**, "**how about I
ring the doorbell, go inside, and get
made into a handbag?**"

"**How are you going to rescue COW if you
are a handbag?**" asks **Duck**, rolling his eyes.
"**Come on, think seriously!**"

I knows what will help my thinking be
more serious – another sweetcorn. I reaches
up to pluck a really big, juicy-looking one.
But just as I does, I sees the scariest thing:
A HUGE **FARMER**!!

WE IS IN BIG TROUBLE!!!!

I has to say **Farmers** from the Other side is very strange looking. His head is huge, and he has straw sticking out of his ears. He stares straight ahead. Maybe he hasn't seen me? I creeps backwards as quietly as I can and bumps into **Ki-Ki**, who lets out a squawk.

The **Farmer** may not have seen us, but now he will have heard us. I throws myself down

on the ground and pulls **Ki-Ki** with me.
Duck throws himself down too.

"**What is it, Pig?**" he whispers.

"There's a **Farmer** in the field!!!" I
whispers back, pointing at him.

Ki-Ki starts laughing. So does **Duck**. I
thinks maybe **Ki-Ki's** madness
has rubbed off on him.

"Why is you both
laughing?" I whispers.
"This is not funny.
This is serious."

Ha! Ha!

Ha! Ha!

"**This is not
serious,**" says **Ki-Ki**, laughing so hard
that little tears pour down his flappy
cheeks. "**This is a Scarecrow!**"

I thinks maybe Scarecrow is the word for **Farmer** on the Other Side. I doesn't understand why **Duck** and **Ki-Ki** is not worried.

"It's OK," says **Duck**. "He's not a real **Farmer**; he's a fake. **Farmers** make them out of straw and old clothes and put them in their fields to scare off greedy animals that try to steal their crops – and it, er, seems to have worked..."

Now **Duck** is being rude. I would never say stuff like that to him!!!

"**I've got an idea!!**" says **Ki-Ki**, hopping up and down. "**How about we play dressing up with the Scarecrow's clothes?**"

"We are here to rescue **COW**," says **Duck** angrily, "**NOT to play games**."

"**It's not a game; it's a disguise!** IVANNA **won't let us in, but she might if we were a Farmer. Pig, you can be the legs, Duck the middle and I, of course, as I can speak a bit of Farmer and am very beautiful, will be the head**."

"**You speak Farmer?**" asks **Duck**, looking rather surprised.

"**Oh, yes - just you watch!**" says **Ki-Ki**. I is going to have to stop writing now, as I need to practise being a **Farmer's** bottom. And it is impossible to write and do that as the same time.

Time Till We Is All Handbags: AAAARGHH!!!!!!!!!!

Hello.

Being a **Farmer** is VERY hard. I has to stand on two trotters. This takes all my concentration. To begin with we wobbles all over the place, but the more we practises, the better I gets. Once I can walk in a straight line, we puts on the disguise and heads out of the cornfield and towards the house. **Duck** is really not happy. He says that for a ball of feathers, **Ki-Ki** is surprisingly heavy, and that if we don't hurry up, he'll be a very flat **Duck**.

I tries to go as fast as I can. There is a small hole in the **Farmer** shirt so I can see where we is going. I peeks out and sees the biggest gates ever with two enormous white pillars on each side. On one pillar is a little silver box with a button in the middle of it. **Ki-Ki** says we needs to press it to get in, so I walks up to it and **Ki-Ki** reaches a wing out through the **Farmer** shirt sleeve and pushes it.

A black box on the top of the pillar makes a whirring noise and points down at us. **"See See Tee Vee,"** says **Duck**, or at least that's what I think he says. It's hard to tell 'cos his flappy feet is covering my ears.

Ki-Ki looks up at the box and waves a **Farmer** arm. The See See Tee Vee whirrs around a bit more. Nothing happens.

Maybe IVANNA is too clever and can see who we really is!

Ki-Ki waves again. We waits some more. Finally, with a loud shudder, the gates starts to open. I lets out a huge sigh of relief. It's so massive it almost unbalances **Duck** and **Ki-Ki**.

We steadies ourselves and walks up towards MAISON MORBEEDE. It's the biggest house I has ever seen. It doesn't have a garden; it just has sand and a few nasty-looking spiky plants. I sees the Bubble Tractor parked on the roof. Luckily I can no longer smell the bad smell; the wind must be blowing in a different direction.

The scared butterflies in my tummy starts to beat their wings super hard. What if these is the last steps I ever takes?

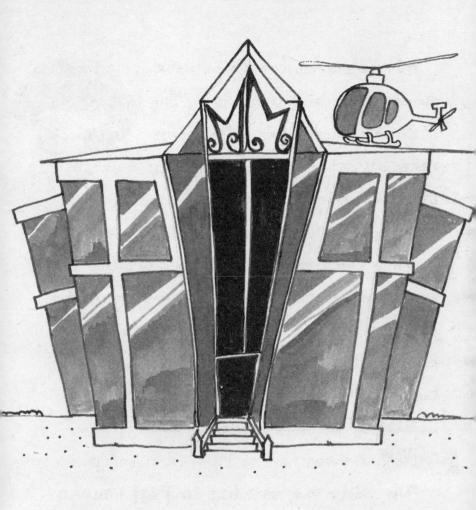

IVANNA is in there and I knows she does horrible things to the animals she captures.

As we reaches the front door, it swings open, and there is IVANNA.

Even though I knows she lives here, I is still shocked to see her. She is even more ugly and orange close up. She is still wearing the same horrible black coat and sunglasses what she was wearing at the show — I wonders if she ever takes them off. I starts to shake. I can feel **Duck's** feet trembling on my ears, but **Ki-Ki** doesn't seem frightened at all.

"**Hello**," he says in Pig.

IVANNA moves her nasty face closer to his.

"**Oh, silly me, talking in Pig! I mean gee-gaa-gad-guuu**," he says, making some very odd noises.

IVANNA snarls.

"I knew it," whispers **Duck**, "**he can't speak Farmer!**"

Ki-Ki continues, only a little bit louder. IVANNA looks us up and down. The corner of her nasty little mouth curls up. She slowly nods, like a thought has popped into her head.

"VEEE, VAAA, VAAAA!" she says, and signals with her arm for us to come inside.

Duck was wrong; **Ki-Ki's Farmer** works. He must know the different kind they speak over here. I is not sure **Duck** can believe it either as I hears him whisper, "**Blimey!**"

IVANNA'S house is AMAZING. Everything is either white and shiny, or gold and shiny.

"**Tell her to take us to COW**," **Duck** whispers.

Ki-Ki makes more noises, and IVANNA leads us through an enormous room full of handbags. Long shelves of them runs around the room from floor to the ceiling; there is bags of every size and colour. But that's not all; the floor is covered in huge glass rectangles with individual bags standing on top of them. These bags looks more special than the ones on the shelves — they is much more sparkly.

"**Beautiful!**" whispers **Ki-Ki**. "**I think I might cry.**"

I thinks I might be sick! I is never letting IVANNA turn **COW** into one of these!

IVANNA opens a door to another room,

and the nasty smell I smelt up on the hill hits
my nose. I wants to hold my trotter over
my snout, but I can't 'cos I is holding on to

Duck's feet. I has no option but to follow her inside. This time it's not bags what is on the walls – it's saws and knives and all sorts of other sharp things. They shines under a large light what hangs from the

ceiling. IVANNA looks at us and runs her hand over a particularly big knife. All the tiny hairs on my body stands on end.

Down one side is a large wooden table that looks like a big version of the one what **Farmer** was going to chip-chop me up on. Laid out on it is even more sharp and pointy tools. My stomach does a scared somersault. I so wants to run away, but we has to get to **COW**.

At the end of the room is a black metal door. IVANNA takes a gold key out of her pocket and opens it. The room on the other side is very dark. There is only one small window in the ceiling. A beam of light shines down on an old **Farmer** bed what is on the floor. On top of the bed I can just make out a large black lump.

"**boooooooooo-mooooooooo...**" says the lump.

IVANNA flicks on the lights. It's **COW**!! And she's covered in red!!! For a moment I panics and thinks it's blood, but then I realizes it's red pen lines in the shape of handbags.

IVANNA has drawn them all over her!

COW looks up at us. A little tear trickles down the side of her face. I wants to tell her it will all be OK and that we has come

to save her, but
I can't 'cos I is
pretending to be a
Farmer.

Ki-Ki suddenly gets VERY excited. He starts flapping our **Farmer** arms and making even more crazy noises. I guesses he must be super happy we has found **COW** too. But then he does something VERY BAD!

He grabs the front of the **Farmer** shirt we is wearing and flings it open!

"WHAT IS YOU DOING???" I shouts, trying to pull the shirt back around us. But it's too late, IVANNA has seen us. She lets out a little laugh. She doesn't even look surprised. I is terrified.

"Don't worry, Pig, you'll thank me for this, I promise," says **Ki-Ki**, happily clapping the **Farmer's** hands together. "**Oh, IVANNA!**" he says, gabbling at a hundred miles an hour, "it's me, your faithful **Ki-Ki**. You know, the one who helps you find all the lucky animals that you turn into beautiful handbags. You always fly off and forget me, but I found my own way here. Hooray! And I brought this Pig with me. Look at his wonderful skin — there is so much of it. And the Duck, with a bit of work, will make a lovely purse. Now, IVANNA, after all I have done for you, will you turn me into one of your wonderful handbags too? I beg you!!"

IVANNA throws her head back and lets out a huge laugh. "VA! VA! VA!" Then she grabs **Ki-Ki** by the neck and plucks him off **Duck's** shoulders. She squeezes his neck so hard I thinks his head might actually pop.

"**Oh, so sorry, mistress,**" says **Ki-Ki** in a voice even higher and more squeaky than his normal one. "**I slipped into Pig again, how silly of me. What I was saying was, gibble, gab, gob, gub...**"

He points his wing at me, just like he pointed it at **COW** at the show, and makes the same odd noises again. IVANNA looks at him, then looks at us. I don't know if she can understand, but she knows what he's trying to say. And what he's trying to say is, **"WOULDN'T THEY MAKE LOVELY HANDBAGS?"**

IVANNA throws **Ki-Ki** to the floor and starts rubbing her hands, just like she did the time she saw **COW**. Now I gets it. She wasn't cold. She was just thinking about turning her into a handbag. And now she is thinking about TURNING ME INTO ONE TOO!!!!!

"NO, **Ki-Ki**, HOW COULD YOU?" I cries. "YOU KNEW ALL WE WANTED TO DO WAS RESCUE **COW**, NOT BECOME HANDBAGS AS WELL!"

"**I just want to make** IVANNA **happy**," squeaks **Ki-Ki**, looking up at her adoringly.

"**Oh, Pig, what fools we've been**," mutters **Duck** under his breath.

"I thought you was our friend!" I says.

"**Friend?**" squeaks **Ki-Ki**. "**No one has ever called me fr-**"

But before he can finish, IVANNA boots him across the floor. I watches as he skids past us.

"**—ieeeend**," he finishes as he hits the wall with a thump.

139

"VA! VA! VA!" laughs IVANNA, pointing a nasty, long finger at him. Ki-Ki looks up, confused, his eyes rolls around and his head flops to the floor.

IVANNA looks at **Duck** and me. Her horrible little mouth twists into a strange shape, which is half happy and half very evil. She slides her hand into her coat pocket, pulls out this strange silver thing and points it at me.

"**OH NO!**" says **Duck**, gripping even tighter to my ears. "**SHE'S GOT A TRANQUILLIZER GUN! RUN, PIG, RUUUUUN!!!!**"

I spins around and is about to head for the door when I hears a little pop noise and something hits my bottom. It stings like a

swarm of bees. I turns around
to see what has made the pain.

There, stuck in my
bottom, is a little arrow
thing with a fuzzy red
end. It's gone straight
through the **Farmer**
trousers and into me. For
a moment everything is
OK, but then the room

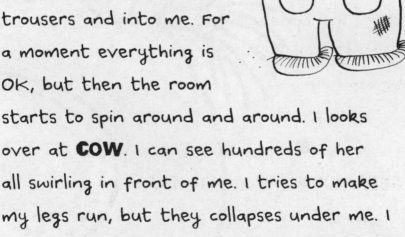

starts to spin around and around. I looks
over at **COW**. I can see hundreds of her
all swirling in front of me. I tries to make
my legs run, but they collapses under me. I
falls to the floor and everything goes black.

Handbag Time: Right Now.
Oh No!!!!!!!!!!

The Cow-Mazing Escape

Hello.

Only joking!

I is not a Pig-shaped handbag. I is still a Pig-shaped Pig.

When I opens my eyes, I is lying on the floor of the dark room, and **Duck** and **COW** is looking down at me. I looks around in a panic for IVANNA and **Ki-Ki**, but they're not here. **COW** gives me a big lick.

"**woc turnip, pig ok**," she says. She means happy. Turnips and happiness is the same in Pig.

I tries to stand up, but my legs is all wobbly. Out of the corner of my eye I

catches a glimpse of something on my belly.
I has got red-pen handbags drawn all over
me – just like **COW**!!!
I stumbles and falls
back down.

"**Take it easy**,"
says **Duck**. "ǏVᴧNNᴧ
**knocked you out with a tranquillizer – you've
been asleep for a while**."

I tries to remember what happened, but
my head feels very foggy.

"**She's locked us in here with COW and she's
taken the double-crossing traitor Ki-Ki with
her**."

As **Duck** says **Ki-Ki's**, name **COW** blows
steam out through her nose and pounds the

ground with her foot. Now I remember – it's **Ki-Ki's** fault we is in this terrible pickle.

"I told **COW** all about him," says **Duck**. "She's not happy." He turns to her and slowly motions with his wings. "**Calm down, COW, we don't have time to be angry; we have to get out of here. Now I am sure Pig is OK, it's time I shared my brilliant escape plan with you both.**"

How exciting! **Duck** has an escape plan. I can't wait to hear what it is.

COW calms herself as **Duck** continues. "**The only way out that I**

can see is through the window in the ceiling."

I looks up at the window. I can sees the moon and a couple of stars. I must have been asleep for a while.

"I propose that I fly up there, push it open, climb out, then locate the key that unlocks this door."

I waits for more, but that's all his plan is. It doesn't sound very brilliant to me. It sounds dangerous.

"What if IVANNA catches you?" I says.

Duck shrugs. **"You got a better idea?"**

Annoyingly I doesn't. So I watches as **Duck** flies up to the window. He gives it a push. It makes a creaking noise, but nothing happens.

147

"Drat!" he calls back down to us. **"It's locked. Maybe it's not such a brilliant plan after all**."

I wants to say "I told you so", but I knows that would not be very helpful.

"where's woc?" says **COW**.

"Really, COW? Now is not the time!" says **Duck**, giving the window another big shove.

"no. woc help break. woc climb up, like where's woc!" she says, walking over to the wall and rearing up on her back legs.

With her front legs, **COW** reaches up the wall and pushes her hooves into the small cracks between the bricks. Then she lifts up her back legs and, one by one, places

them into the small
cracks too.
She takes
a deep
breath
and pushes
herself up.
Her whole body
trembles; I
can see all her
muscles bulging. I can't

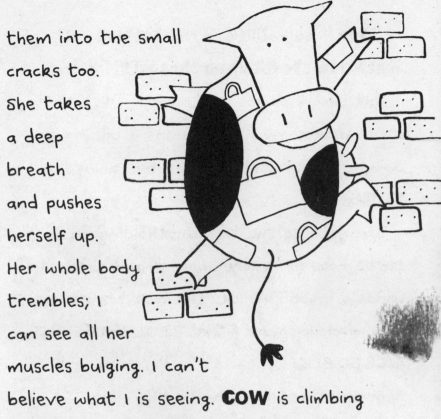

believe what I is seeing. **COW** is climbing
the wall like a spider. A **COW**-spider. A
CIDER. I would tell her my clever name,
but I doesn't want to make her laugh — she
might lose concentration and fall off.

"**Wow!**" says **Duck**. "**Free climbing – so that's how she got up on the roof!**"

She slowly climbs up towards **Duck**. Every move makes my heart jumps a bit higher up my throat. Please don't be falling, **COW**...

She gets to the top and, holding on with three hooves, reaches across and gives the window a good whack. The lock breaks and the window opens. **COW** REALLY IS SUPER INCREDIBLE.

She clutches back on to the wall.

"**woc has big parsnip**," she says and whispers something into **Duck's** ear. He nods.

"What is it?" I asks. I hates not knowing secrets.

"**COW would like you to sit on the bed**," says **Duck**.

I follows his instructions. I guesses, just like with the **Sandals'** roof, **COW** is not so good at the climbing down bit, and she wants me to catch her. Surely she knows she's too heavy?!

"Is you sure this is a good idea?" I shouts. "I is not sure I is going to be strong enough. No offence, **COW**."

"**Don't worry, you'll be fine**," says **Duck**. "**Just shift over a little bit more. That's right. OK, ready, COW?**"

COW lets go and falls towards me. I closes my eyes, reaches out my arms and waits for her to land.

But **COW** doesn't land in my arms.

With a loud BUMPFFFF, she lands right next to me.

The springs in the **Farmer** bed goes BOING! and I feels myself being thrown up into the air. I opens my eyes as,

WHOOOSH!

I flies out through the window. Up I flies, into the night sky. Woooo-hoooo! Clever **COW** has turned me into a Pig-rocket.

"I IS A PROCKET!" I cries as I zooms up.

But I is not flying for long. Soon I is falling very fast towards the ground. ARGHHHHH!

Maybe **COW'S** plan is not so great after all. But then, SPLASH! I lands in a large pond. I feels myself hit the bottom, then I bounces back up to the surface. I tries to catch my breath as disgusting-tasting water flies up my nose and into my mouth. I paddles my legs, just like **Duck** told me to the time I fell into the **Sheeps'** pond. I feels them touch the bottom. I can stand up!

Duck lands in the water next to me.

"Good job you landed in the shallow end," he says.

Big Farty-Trouble

Hello.

You will not be believing this:
Farmers has ponds, just like **Ducks**.
How bonkers is that?! **Duck** says they
is called swimming pools and only posh
Farmers has them. IVANNA'S is in her
back garden, just behind her enormous glass
house, and I landed in it.

The water is nice and warm — not like
Duck Pond. I wishes we had more time; it
would be the perfect place to see if I could
break my "fart bubble" record.

"Right," says **Duck**, hopping out of the pool
and flattening himself against the grass,

155

"commando crawl. Follow me!" I wonders
where **Duck** has been learning all this
signalling and crawling stuff. It's not like he
goes on dangerous missions all the time!

Whatever commando crawl is, it is not
easy if you has a big belly. I is glad we
doesn't have to go far to reach the house.

We spies IVANNA through one of the huge
windows. She's sitting on a pink sofa watching
a big black box what has moving pictures on it.

"Great, she's busy watching Tee Vee," says **Duck**.

I notices her feet is resting on something big and feathery. IT's **Ki-Ki**!! IVANNA has killed **Ki-Ki**, stuffed him and turned him into a stool!!

Ha! Ha! For a minute I thinks this is very funny, but then I starts to feel sorry for him. **Ki-Ki** wanted to be a handbag, not a footrest.

Duck nudges me and points to a gold key on a little table in the corner of the room. I nods; we just needs to get inside and I can get it. I is a good key-stealer. I may be big, but I is also super sneaky.

We crawls a bit further along the wall until we gets to a big glass back door.

I presses my bottom up against the glass and pushes. I opens it just enough for **Duck** and me to squeeze through. I takes a deep breath and creeps towards the living room, **Duck's** feet going flip-flap, flip-flap on the shiny floor.

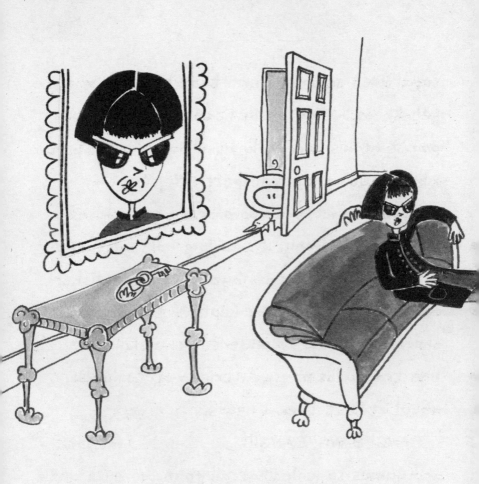

The living-room door is open just enough
for us to peer inside. To get the keys, we is
going to have to sneak along behind IVANNA'S

sofa. **Duck** signals to me that he is going to get them. I shakes my head — bad idea. I points at his noisy, flippy-flappy feet, then I bends down and whispers, "**Hop on.**"

I creeps into the room like a super-stealthy Pig-pony. It's boiling hot. IVANNA has a huge fire burning. Maybe that is why her month is so small; the heat of the fire has shrivelled it up. I wonders if she still has the tranquillizer gun. I tries not to think about it, but then I hears,

BANG! BANG! BANG!!

I jumps so high that all four of my trotters leaves the ground. **Duck** loses his grip and falls to the floor with a thunk.

"**It's OK,**" mouths **Duck**, pointing at the box

in the corner. **"It was a film on the Tee Vee."**

We is right behind IVANNA. I hears her move. Maybe she heard us? We both curls up into the smallest balls we can. The problem with curling into a small ball is that it pushes around all the wind inside your tummy. I squeezes my bottom as tightly as I can. Please don't fart, I begs it; now would be a very BAD time for even a very small mole-sounding one. But my bottom isn't listening, and a snake one hisses out. For a moment I thinks it doesn't smell, but then it reaches my nose; it's a super-stealthy stonking stinker. I tries to breathe in all the air around me to stop it spreading, but I can't.

Duck gives me a "WHAT HAVE YOU DONE, PIG????" look. All I can do is a little "sorry" shrug. We waits for my tiny, evil fart to hit IVANNA'S nose, but it's not IVANNA who smells it first.

"**OMG!**" I hear **Ki-Ki** cry.

I can't believe it. **Ki-Ki** is ALIVE!

Then I hears IVANNA scream in pain. I

peeks around the side
of the sofa to see
what has happened.
The not-dead
Ki-Ki has passed
out on the floor,
dumping IVANNA'S
feet into the fire.
She jumps up and screeches,
then kicks **Ki-Ki** so hard that
he flies over the sofa, landing
right next to us. The fall brings
him back round.

I looks down at him. Some of his feathers
is burnt. I expects him to start shouting
for IVANNA, but he doesn't. All three of

us does NOTHING. IVANNA lets out another
annoyed screech, turns off the Tee Vee and
storms out of the room. As soon as she is
gone **Ki-Ki** bursts into tears.

The Bonkers Bird's Back

Hello.

I has never seen an animal cry as much as **Ki-Ki**. I has no idea how he has so much water inside his body.

"I...am...so... s...s...sorry," he says between sobs.

"Sorry!!" I says in my crossest whisper. I feels all hot inside – VERY hot and VERY angry. "We're about to be turned into handbags and it's all your fault!!!!!!!"

"I know, I've been such a foolish bird. I – I – thought that the more I

helped IVANNA, the more she would love
me. But I was wrong — she was just
using me. I didn't understand what
true friendship was, until you showed
me. And now I realize, I don't want to
be a handbag ... I just want to be ...
a friend."

Ki-Ki collapses into a sobbing, feathery
ball on the floor. As I looks down at him the
angry, burning feeling inside me starts to
change. I starts to feel sad.

Something about what he said reminds
me of my old Farmer. I thought
he loved me, but then Duck told me he
just wanted to eat me for his dinner. I
remembers how terrible I felt when I found

out — how I wanted to curl up in a ball and cry, just like **Ki-Ki**. I doesn't know why I feels bad for him after what he has done, but I does.

"I understands," I says. "I loved a nasty **Farmer** once too."

"**Really?**" says **Ki-Ki**. "**Does that mean you can, maybe, one day, forgive me?**"

I thinks for a moment. "Hmmmm, maybe."

"**Yes, maybe,**" says **Duck**. "**If you help us get out of here!**"

Ki-Ki jumps to his feet and wipes his wet face with his wing. "**Yes!**" he nods. "**I can do that. Grab that key and follow me.**"

Duck grabs the key off the table with his beak while **Ki-Ki** listens carefully at the door. **"She's gone upstairs,"** he whispers. **"Come on, this way."**

We tiptoes back through the house to the door of **COW'S** prison. **Duck** hops up on my back and puts the key in the lock.

"It's us, **COW**!" I says as the door swings open. "We really is going to rescue you this time."

COW comes bounding out, but stops suddenly when she sees **Ki-Ki**. She lowers her head and lets out a loud snort. Steam comes out of her nostrils, just like before.

"**Ki-Ki salt!**" she says and scrapes her front foot on the ground.

"Yes," I says, "**Ki-Ki** has been very BAD, but now he wants to help us. If he tricks us again, you can be doing whatever you likes to him!"

"**She can?**" squeaks **Ki-Ki**.

COW stops scraping her foot and lets out a final burst of steam. She gives **Ki-Ki** the fiercest look I has ever seen. He lets out a little whimper.

"**OK**," whispers **Duck**, "**let's head back to the cornfield. Once we're there we should be safe.**"

Goodnight, Ivanna Hertchew!

Hello.

In the front of my diary, when I is saying that I thinks my stories will just be ordinary ... well, I was definitely wrong. When I tells you what I is about to tell you, I thinks you will be agreeing that I should put an "extra" in before the ordinary: extra-ordinary. Ha! Ha! I is getting very clever with my words.

But I is still very silly too. I almost totally messes up our escape.

Ki-Ki listens out for IVANNA whilst we sneaks out the back door. He says he is pretty sure she has gone to bed.

As we creeps around the side of the house, I spies the cornfield. Yummy, I thinks, imagining all the delicious corns inside it. I starts walking a bit faster as my tummy is super excited to start eating them. I is in such a hurry that I doesn't see a big metal bin what is in front of me. CRASH! I knocks it straight over, and super-delicious garliky slops spills out all over the floor. Perhaps I has time for just one little bite? But then a huge, bright light suddenly shines around me and a horrible honking noise goes: AHOO-ARRR! AHOO-ARRR! AHOO-ARRR!

I tries to escape the light, but it follows me wherever I runs. Then I hears an even

more horrible noise — IVANNA is leaning out
of an upstairs window, screeching and
squawking and flapping her arms like a
crazy Blackbird.

"**This way, Pig!!**" shouts **Duck**, and I chases
the others towards the big gate. As I gets

closer, it starts to close. **COW** makes it through, then **Duck**, then **Ki-Ki**, but the gap gets smaller and smaller.

"**QUICK, PIG!!!**" shouts **Duck**.

I tries to make my legs go faster, but they can't. I watches as the gate slams shut. But just as it does, **Ki-Ki** throws himself into the gap and pushes his wings out, holding the two gates apart.

I can see from his face that it is taking all his strength. I dives over the top of him. I feels the gate scrape against the side of my belly. I just makes it through.

CLANG! The gates slams closed. I looks around to see if **Ki-Ki** is OK. He's trapped, hanging floppily, not moving.

I runs over to him. "**Ki-Ki**," I says, "is you alive?"

He lifts up his neck and I sees that it is not his body what is squished in the gate, it's his tail.

"**Leave me**," he says. "**I am worthless — save yourselves**."

"You is not worthless," I says.

"You just saved my life!!"

I grabs his feathery body gently in my mouth and gives him a big tug. He's really stuck. I gives him an even bigger tug. I hears a faint ripping sound, then **Ki-Ki** suddenly comes free. We both falls backwards on to the floor. I looks up at the gate. **Ki-Ki** is no longer trapped, but his prize-winning tail feathers still is. They hangs there, blowing in the breeze.

I expects him to start screaming, but instead he calmly says, "**It doesn't matter. I don't deserve a nice tail after what I've done!**" Tears form in his eyes, but before they can plop out we hears, WUMP! WUMP! WUMP!

There above us, rising into the sky, is
IVANNA'S Bubble Tractor. A bright light, just
like the one what chased me across the
garden, shines down from it.

"THE CORNFIELD, NOW!!!!" shouts **Duck**.
We runs and dives into the corn, hiding
under the tall stalks as the light follows.
The corn is so thick that the beam can't
reach us.

Phew! We is safe.

I peers up through the stalks, hoping to
see IVANNA fly away. But instead I sees her
reach her arm out and drop something
bright. It falls slowly through the air, then
lands. WUMPHHH! Huge flames leaps up
behind us.

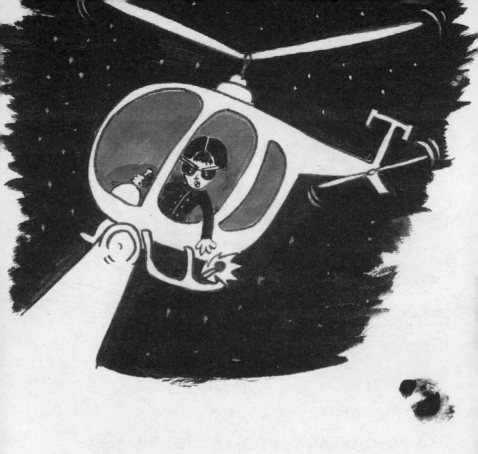

"SHE'S SET THE FIELD ON FIRE!!!!" I
shouts. "RUN FOR YOUR LIVES!!!"

We all crashes through the tall stalks,
trying to get away. I can hear the cornfield
burning behind me. CRACK, FIZZLE,

CRACK, CRACK, FIZZLE, POP! it goes.
I can smells it too. I has to say, burning
sweetcorn smells quite yummy.

I looks around to see where everyone else
is, but it's very dark and the smoke from
the fire is getting thicker and thicker. It

fills my mouth, stings my eyes and makes my chest burn. I starts to cough and splutter and my legs starts to wobble.

I doesn't want us to die like this, roasted in a burning field. We has made it so far — we has reached the Other Side and rescued **COW**. Dying doesn't seem fair. Tears starts to pour out of my eyes. I is not sure whether this is because I is sad or because the smoke is making them water. My legs starts to feel like they can't run any more. It takes all my strength to carry on. My coughing gets worse and worse. I stumbles and falls, I tumbles and rolls, and then I is falling, falling through the air.

BOOMPH! I lands on my back, and all the air flies out of me. I can't breathe. All I can see is black and stars. There is no corn around me any more.

Then **Duck** lands on top of me, and **Ki-Ki** and **COW** rolls coughing next to me.

"**OMG!**" pants **Ki-Ki**. "**We're back on the beach.**"

I looks around. He's right. The flames from the cornfield light up the beach and make the sea shine. Somehow we has all made it out alive. I wants to give everyone a big hug, but my legs just isn't long enough.

But then, WUMP! WUMP! WUMP! the Bubble
Tractor rises up over the flaming field.

Hanging underneath it is the large net what IVANNA whisked **COW** away in.

NOW SHE'S COMING TO WHISK US ALL AWAY!!!!!

IVANNA is shouting into this large cone-shaped thing what makes her voice very loud. We all freezes, not sure what to do.

"What's she saying, **Duck**?" I shouts over the noise of the Bubble Tractor.

"She's saying she is going to make you and COW into some

lovely bags, she is going to use my feathers to stuff something and she is going to serve **Ki-Ki** up with some delicious cranberry sauce," he shouts back.

COW and **Ki-Ki** both starts to tremble. Even **Duck** looks scared. The Bubble Tractor swoops down towards us. Sand blows everywhere. It flies into my eyes and up my nose.

"VAR! VAR! VAR!" I hears IVANNA'S laugh. We all huddles into a ball, covering our mouths and eyes.

In my head I tries to think of something nice to make the horrible thing what is happening go away. If this is the end, I wants to finish with some happy thoughts

in my head. I pictures **Mr Sandal**; he's
singing his special song to me. I hears his
words in my head:

Piggy, Piggy, we love you,
Piggy, old chap!
Duck, old bean!
COW, old stick!
Ki-Ki, old chestnut!
Over here! Over here!

This is not how the song goes, I thinks. That
is NOT **Mr Sandal's** voice. I peeks through my
trotters and sees the most amazing thing.
It's Old Celia, the submarine and
standing on top of her is *The Captain*. He is

frantically waving at us. "*Come on, chaps and chapesses,*" he shouts, "*no time to lose!!*"

As we gets to our feet, I hears the big net swoosh over the top of us. It skims across **COW'S** back, but doesn't catch her. We staggers through the blowing sand

and into the sea. **Ki-Ki** gets to Old Celia first, and he helps **COW** scramble up the little ladder on the side. *The Captain* opens a big metal door on the top and they both disappears inside.

I hears the Bubble Tractor coming back again as I splashes into the water and, just like **COW**, scrambles up on to Old Celia. I looks back for **Duck**; he's in the water, paddling as fast as he can.

I sees the net lower behind him. Whooosh! It scoops him up. IVANNA screeches some strange **Farmer** words what sounds like, "HAR! HAR! NUVO DUVAY."

Duck tries to struggle free, but his foot gets caught. He dangles upside down in the air, his wings flapping madly. He starts screaming. I has NEVER heard **Duck** scream before. It's horrible.

"**DUCK!**" I cries. "**DUCK, NO!**"

The net swings over the submarine, just above my head. I has only one option: I leaps up and grabs hold of one of **Duck's** wings. I is not going to let IVANNA take my best friend.

The Bubble Tractor sweeps up into the air. I holds on to **Duck's** wing, hoping that my weight will pull his foot free, but it's too tangled. My trotter starts to slip.

I grips harder, trying to hold on. But I can't.
I can't hold on any longer.

Suddenly I is falling through the air,
Duck's frightened face getting
further and further
away.

With a very
painful CRASH! I
lands bottom-
first on the
top of a small
button what
is sticking
out of the
top of Old
Celia.

I crushes it flat. Old Celia makes a terrible groaning noise like something bad has happened.

No, no, I thinks, I can't be losing my best friend.

But then the most bonkers thing in the whole wide world happens. With a loud groan, two metal doors opens up, and out of Old Celia flies this long, thin rocket.

Whooooosh!

It goes up into the air.

BOOOOOOOOOOOOOMMMMMMMM!

IVANNA'S Bubble Tractor turns into a
big, yellow ball of flames. Bits of it flies
everywhere and something black and
flaming flaps down into the sea next
to me.

It's IVANNA'S horrible black coat. It lands in the water with a loud HISSSS. Her melted sunglasses plops down next to it. Goodbye, horrible IVANNA HERTCHEW. The world is a better place without you, your coat and your silly sunglasses! Ha! Ha! Ha!

The blast blows **Duck** out of the net. I only just catches him before he lands painfully on Old Celia too. I looks down at him in my arms. My best friend is safe; I is so happy I could cry like **Ki-Ki**. For a moment I thought I was never going to see him again.

"Oh, **Duck**," I says, "I loves ..."

I suddenly realizes what I is saying. I has never told **Duck** I loves him. What if he thinks I is a big softie Pig?!

"... Old Celia!" I says, popping him down and giving the submarine a pat.

"Well, Pig, I love you. You just saved my life!"

DUCK JUST TOLD ME HE LOVES ME! HOW AMAZING IS THAT?! I is just about to tell him that of course I loves him too, much more than Old Celia, when *The Captain* comes over.

"Well, well, well," he says. *"I always wondered what that button did. Didn't know*

Old Celia had it in her." We looks at each other and starts to laugh. **COW** and **Ki-Ki** pokes their heads out of the hatch and starts laughing too.

"*Now, I think that's quite enough adventure for one day,*" says The Captain. "*All aboard and I'll give you a lift back to Blighty – or, as you landlubbers call it, home.*"

Homeseyday

Hello.

Old Celia really is quite amazing. I was never knowing that it is possible to go under the water without having to hold your breath. But that is just what a submarine lets you do. I wishes I had a mini one what I could use in **Duck Pond**!

The Captain has these huge maps what shows him where all the rivers and seas is. **Duck** studies them carefully and works out that *The Captain* can take us nearly all the way home. There is a big river what runs up close to where the **Farm** is.

I is SOOOO happy that we has rescued

COW. In fact, everyone seems happy – everyone apart from **Ki-Ki**. He sits quietly in the corner by himself, staring at his odd-shaped **Turkey** toes.

"What's wrong?" I asks. "You should be happy; we is going home!"

"I don't have a home, Pig," he says, **"and I don't have any friends. I am a bad, bad Ki-Ki."**

"That's not true," I says. "You was a bad **Ki-Ki**, but you helped us escape. I'd be a handbag if it wasn't for you!"

"Ki-Ki help woc on bus," says **COW**, smiling.

"**Bus?**" says **Ki-Ki**, looking a little confused.

"**She means sub ... submarine,**" says **Duck**, laughing. "**I think you have learnt your lesson. You have found a way back into our Good Book.**"

Now I feels very confused. I didn't know we has a Good Book too. Maybe **Duck** keeps it secret, like I does with my diaries? Why hasn't I seen it? I guess because he keeps it in his house.

"If you promises to stay good," I says, "then we will let you share our home."

"**Oh, I do, I do,**" he says, clapping his wings together and bouncing up and down.

The Captain takes us up the river until it gets too shallow for Old Celia. We thanks

him for all his help. As we climbs out,
Ki-Ki stops, takes off his necklace, places
it around *The Captain*'s neck and gives him a
little kiss on the cheek.

"**My hero!**" he says, batting his funny
little **Turkey** eyelashes.

The Captain blushes so much he goes red
from top to toe. "*Well, er, you are too kind,
m'dear, really,*" he says, patting the gift.
"*I hope one day our paths may cross
again. Until that time, though,
toodle-pip, tutty-bye and
cheerio!*"

And with a flippery
salute, he shuts the
hatch and Old Celia

disappears back under the water.

Duck points out that **COW** and I still has handbags drawn all over us. He suggests we has a little bath in the river to get rid of them. He helps us rub them off with his feathery bottom – it really tickles!

We only has a short walk back to the **Farm**, but with every step, I worries more and more about what **Mr and Mrs Sandal** is going to do when they sees us. What if they never forgives us? What if we never gets back in their Good Book?

We reaches the gate and I looks up at the house. The blue sheet has gone and the roof no longer has a hole in it. This makes me feel a bit better. We doesn't know quite what to do, so we all heads over to **Duck Pond** and hangs out like nothing has happened.

No sooner has we all reached the pond than **Mrs Sandal** comes running out of the house screaming and shouting. For a moment my heart sinks. Perhaps she is still upset with us? But then I see that she is smiling – her shouts is happy ones. I is SOOOOOO pleased to see her. **Mr Sandal** follows her out. He looks happy too and a little surprised.

Ki-Ki nervously hides behind me while the **Sandals**

gives us lots of pats and strokes, all the time chatting away in **Farmer**. Duck translates.

"**Mrs Sandal says she thought someone had kidnapped us,**" says **Duck**, laughing. "**Mr Sandal told her not to be so silly. He says we probably just went for a wander and a graze and got a bit lost.**"

Ha! Ha! Ha! We all starts laughing. **Ki-Ki** lets out a huge **Turkey** laugh: "**Gobble-ga! Gobble-ga!**"

Mrs Sandal peers behind me and jumps back in surprise. I wonders for a moment if she has never seen a **Turkey**. **Ki-Ki** clears his throat and starts talking just like he did to IVANNA.

"**Gub, gib, gabble, gub, gib Ki-Ki**," he says.

"Gobble, gobble," replies **Mrs Sandal** laughing.

Ki-Ki looks a bit confused. "**I hate to break it to you**," says **Duck**, laughing, "**but I don't think Farmers understand you.**"

"But IVANNA?"

"Nope," says Duck, "you just thought she understood you!"

"Oh," says Ki-Ki with a sad sigh. "Well, never mind, hey! It's kind of funny, right? Gib, gab, gabble, gob!"

"Gobble, gobble," say both Mr and Mrs Sandal back, laughing even more.

Ha! Ha! I thinks they likes him.

I doesn't want them to think that there is no room for Ki-Ki, so I tells him he can stay in my house until they finds him a place of his own. I takes him over and shows him inside.

I is so happy to be back. I never thought I would be so pleased to see my bed. I does a little Pig dance – a Piggy-jiggy. Ha! Ha!

I wonders what **Ki-Ki** thinks of my place. I is sure he's never stayed in a Pig house before. I guesses he must like it, 'cos he quickly starts making a little **Turkey** nest.

I is just making myself a Piggy one, ready for a nice big nap, when **COW** and **Duck** pops their heads in.

"Hey, Pig, mind if we join you?" says **Duck**. **"Feels like we could all do with a sleep. And after the adventure we've all had, don't you think it would be nice to have one together?"**

"Yes, please," I says. "I loves sleepovers, or maybe I should say snooze-overs as it's only the afternoon. Ha! Ha! Ha!"

I makes a Piggy nest big enough for all of us. We curls up together. I is soooooooooooooooooo happy.

I gets the feeling that maybe my life will never be just ordinary. I doesn't mind though. As long as I has my friends, slops and farting games, I will always be happy.

I lays my head down. **Ki-Ki** lets me rest it on him. He makes the best pillow ever; I doesn't have to use my trotters any more! Maybe our big, scary adventure wasn't so bad after all. Ha! Ha! Ha!

Lots of Love,
Pig, Duck, COW
and Ki-Ki
xxxx

Read Pig's first top-secret diary!

And don't miss his
super-amazing second diary!

Visit Pig's EXTRA-ORDINARY website diaryofpig.com to find out more about him, ask him questions, discover fun Piggy activities and much much more.